SILENT NIGHT
and Other Stories

BOOK ONE OF THE
KALEIDOSCOPE SERIES

JULIE ROBERTS
Hartslock Publishing

SILENT NIGHT AND OTHER STORIES

Please note that the spelling and grammar in this book are UK English.

Published by **Hartslock Publishing**

TABLE OF CONTENTS

ACKNOWLEDGMENTS

I would like to thank Jeeve Publishing for their support. A special thank you to Nina Harrington for her help in getting this Kaleidoscope series into print.

INTRODUCTION TO THE KALEIDOSCOPE SERIES

My Kaleidoscope series is a mixture of genres. As you turn the last page of a story, I hope you will find the change of lengths and emotions a pleasure to read. Or you may wish to hop around the pages at random. But whatever your choice, I hope you like what you find.

Julie

MOUNTAIN MUSIC

The haunting music of pan pipes drifted over the valley like an echoing mist. It murmured through the trees, flowed down the stream and skipped from rock to rock. Bianca stretched her arms high, swayed to the music and sang with the pipes the words she had written for her lover's melody. Juan was coming to her.

She had discovered the lodge camp on the internet – and for the past month it had been her haven from the western world. Full of happiness and anticipation she hurried along the path towards the one room native cabin hidden within the Peruvian rain forest; furnished with only a chair, mirror, chest of drawers and her netted bed. As she entered she slipped off her sandals and the cool floor felt wonderful, the fresh bed sheets waiting for the night.

'Not yet,' she whispered.

She lifted a fresh gossamer gown from her case and laid it over the chair. With the song still in her head she pulled off her shorts and top and went into the shower. She tilted her face to the sun warmed water and let it stream between her breasts, spread in rivulets across her stomach and run down her legs.

The music was closer, like a breeze warm and sensual. Cooled and still damp she slipped on the halter neck gown, the deep cleft of the bodice reaching to her waist. In the mirror her reflection had lost its paleness. She touched the hair that had taken months to grow back and the auburn tints gleamed in the sunlight coming through the window.

Bianca waited, the music came nearer and her breathing deepened. The notes softened to a flowing lullaby, each as tender as his kiss. His shadow fell across the threshold as perfect as the young man himself. Juan held the pipes to his lips, dark eyes sparkling, olive skin smooth where he'd shaved. He wore a multi coloured shirt and knee-length shorts.

He was beautiful.

'At last, Juan, I have been listening to your music, dancing and singing, waiting for you.'

Juan smiled as he stepped towards her. 'You will always be waiting, and I will always come. It is our destiny.'

'We will not speak of that.' Her words sounded sharp, and she regretted them because tonight was not a time for arguing. 'Come, you must be thirsty from your long walk over the hills. I've had the lodge steward prepare a special supper for us.'

Bianca held out her hand and led him to the thatched veranda. She wound her arms around his neck and kissed him, regaining the magic of his presence. She drew away slightly but he pulled her back.

'That is not enough, I long for much more.' He kissed her with a demanding passion, running his fingers through her soft curls, caressing her bare back. She'd taught him how to please her – and he'd morphed from a caterpillar to a butterfly – from a fumbling youth to a skilful lover.

'Later, my love, let the sun set and the air cool, it will sweeten our needs.'

Juan nodded. 'You have great patience, Bianca.' He moved to the table. 'Wine and a walk through the forest will help.' He handed her an iced glass of wine and they wandered along the winding path between the ferns, their fingers entwined in peaceful harmony.

Juan raised his glass. 'I toast the forest and the stillness of night. The birds have nested; the day animals will sleep and the nocturnal hunters awake. The lamplight from the veranda glows like an oasis, a beacon to lead us back.'

She stopped, sadness washing over her. 'I shall miss this when I go. My time here in the forest has shown me there can be a different life to a world gone crazy.'

'Then stay. Stay with me forever.'

'Oh, Juan, if only I could. Forever is not mine to have. You know that, my love. What we have now is all I can give you.'

'Don't speak so; don't torment me with what I cannot have.'

'Even if I could stay, you are a young man with a life before you. You will take a wife, raise a family and, I hope, sometimes think of us as we are tonight dining on the veranda and making love until the dawn.'

Juan stood silent, his eyes changing to black caverns of despair. 'You can be very cruel, Bianca.'

'Not cruel, Juan, you will realise that one day. Lies would only twist your heart and make you hate me. I couldn't bear that, my love.'

She stepped close and kissed him on each cheek and then his wine-tasting lips. 'It's time to eat. I've ordered oysters and fruit. You will eat like a Greek God with dark, ripe grapes. I have had them flown in especially for you.'

Bianca served from a side table and passed Juan his plate. 'From the great sea you have never seen.' He accepted it without comment.

Bianca wasn't hungry, but she put a few oysters on her plate. 'Now, I will show you how to eat them.' She picked up an oyster and slipped the soft flesh into her mouth, closed her eyes and swallowed; the taste was exquisite.

Juan touched her hand. 'Are they sweeter than my kiss?'

She opened her eyes. 'Nothing can be sweeter than your kiss.' She leant forward and touched his lips with her finger. 'Now it's your turn.'

She watched him take his first taste of one of her world's delicacy. There were plenty of river fish for the local people, but fish brought from the sea? She wanted tonight to be special for Juan, for him to sample something he may never taste again. And he was eating with pleasure, true pleasure, not just pleasing her. She rose and brought the platter to the table and served him more.

He looked at her, his smile betraying much more than a thank you. 'They are wonderful. I will remember the taste forever.'

Such a normal thing to her, but his pleasure filled her with something she couldn't explain. Perhaps it was like giving a child a surprise Christmas gift and seeing the joy light up its face.

Is this how she saw Juan? As a child! No, he was her beautiful lover. But she was forty. She had been twenty, at university, bed-hopping and smoking marijuana when he was born. Her friends would call him her toy-boy and raise their eyebrows, but she felt no shame. Had isolation in this strange land intoxicated her like a drug? Had Juan's musical pan pipes bewitched her? So be it. This was her swansong to life and she'd chosen to take what was left with him.

Juan continued to eat in silence. She wondered what he was thinking. 'Talk to me, Juan.'

His eyes were full of sadness and regret. He lifted the pipes to his lips and played. The haunting notes drifted to her, soft, caressing, like finger-tips rippling down her spine. She closed her eyes, a growing need filling her and she followed Juan's melody as he drew her to their night of love.

'Juan, wake up.' Bianca kissed his slightly parted lips and he opened his eyes. 'It's time for us to part.'

'Yes.' The word was thick with tears. 'You must go and I must return to my home, music and sorrow.'

'We cannot pretend this day wouldn't come. I owe my daughters my last months of life. If I had known this tenderness was waiting for me, I would have come to you sooner. I have no words of comfort, except our lives have been enriched in finding each other.' As she kissed him a knot of regret settled within her, she so wanted to stay and be loved by him.

'I have a promise to ask of you.'

Juan moved and leant on his elbow.

She stroked his cheek with her finger, tracing the line of his jaw. Her words were hard to say, but she wanted him to remember her.

'Love and marry one day. Tell your wife about us and perhaps call your daughter, Bianca?'

Tears slid down Juan's cheeks. She pulled his head close and kissed away his tears. 'I have loved and been loved. I am happy.'

Juan kissed her one more time and left their bed. He dressed and turning to her in the doorway, raised the pipes to his lips and left.

Bianca lay still and listened. Juan's musical notes were clear and beautiful as they faded into the morning sky.

TALKING NUMBERS

The instructions say, "If you want help, phone..."

'Good morning, this is Dye Hard Hair Consultants.

If you want to enquire about our fabulous hair colours, please press 1.

If you want to know about our stockists, press 2.

If you want to know about our full range of products, press 3.

If you want to know how to order a product, press 4.

If you want to speak to a consultant; please press hash and wait.'

The sweet tones of music fill my ears, *Over the sea to Skye...*

I hum along with the tune, this is pleasant and then suddenly, 'Sorry to keep you waiting,' brings me out of my musing.

This has cost me four minutes so far.

Back with, *Over the sea to Skye...*

The window could do with a clean; I could write my name in the dust.

Hey, a van has pulled up across the street at number 51. They're having a new kitchen delivered. Good job I'm sitting here, I would have missed seeing it going in.

'Sorry to keep you waiting,' pipes in an accented lilt.

Six minutes!

A repeat of *Over the sea to Skye...* I'm beginning to hate this lyrical drone.

The new postman looks harassed in the rain; he's just dropped all the envelopes on the wet pavement.

Eight minutes!

At last, a human voice. 'Marie here, Customer Services, how may I help you?'

'Hello, I bought a box of your blonde hair dye...'

'Sorry to butt in, but you need to redial and press option 5. Thank you for calling.'

'But there is no opt...'

She's gone, the stupid girl has gone!

Press redial.

'Good morning, this is Dye Hard Hair Consultants.

If you want to enquire about our fabulous hair colours, please press 1.

...press 2.

...press 3.

...press 4.

If you want to speak to a consultant; please press hash and wait.'

Ten minutes!

And I'm back to square one.

I shout at the handset: 'You must be joking.'

Two can play at putting the receiver down.

I'm not going through all that again. I'll keep my white Granny locks. I'll get a refund. That'll knock their profit down.

SHELDON

Isabelle Courtney looked at the clock on her desk – sixteen hundred hours. It was time to activate Sheldon. She picked up her satellite phone and punched in a code, then dropped it into her travelling bag.

Rising from behind her desk, she went and took her raincoat from a concealed wall cupboard and left.

The rain was heavy as she stepped from the revolving door, but she didn't bother to use her umbrella as she ran up the steps to a waiting monorail train.

It was a blessing her Directorate Building was on the National circuit, a train passed every five minutes. Being Friday, most of the seats were taken, but she found a flip-down one next to the emergency exit. She took a hand-held screen from her bag and turned it on. At last, time for herself, she could finish reading her novel.

The journey would take two and one quarter hours precisely, the train's speed regulated by how long it stopped at each station.

Muss-by-Weir flashed in red, and Isabelle passed her hand across the halt panel. When the train stopped, the door slid aside and she stepped out onto the raised platform and hurried down the steps.

Sheldon waved, waiting beside a low bulbous car.

'Oh, I'm so glad to see you, Sheldon. It's been a monster of a week. I can't wait to get home.'

'Come here.' He pulled Isabelle close and kissed her on the lips. 'Happy Valentine's Day, darling.'

'Thank you for the celebration trinket.' She lifted her arm and the coat sleeve slipped to her elbow. 'Did you spend all your credit points on me?'

'Who else deserves them?' he said, and opened the car door for her.

The ride took only a few minutes and Sheldon parked beside a garden wall. He tapped a code into a screen on his wristband and the house lights blazed from every window.

Isabelle was delighted and silently thanked her ancestors for the inheritance of the twentieth century cottage. There were not many brick and wood properties left. Modern housing consisted of bland and featureless apartments, even in the country.

An hour later, Isabelle looked at her reflection in the mirror as she combed her dark hair and coiled it into a high knot, securing it with a tortoise-shell clip. It had cost a year's worth of working points, but it was something she just had to have. Pulling on a swathe of multi-coloured cloth she belted it round her waist and slipped her feet into soft moon-thread shoes and left the bedroom.

Pausing in the doorway of the dining room, she heard Mozart filling every corner. On the table, laid for two, candles flickered, (but they never dripped wax), and stark white poly-textured plates looked out of place amidst chintz furnishings. Noises came from the kitchen: the pinging of the infra-red oven, the hiss of plastic expanding, and the smell of food. Looking immaculate in a black and white suit, Sheldon came in carrying the dishes.

'I've chilled the wine to your exact liking. It will be a perfect dinner.'

He filled two antique fluted glasses and handed her one. He raised his high and smiled, 'To our last weekend.' Isabelle did not respond, just raised her glass and sipped. 'Shall we eat?' He took her wine-glass and placed it on the table, then pulled back the chair for her.

'Thank you.' It was said with a sigh.

Sheldon served with the expertise of a waiter and the grace of a dancer, and placed her plate in front of her.

He was driving her mad. She gripped the knife and fork like daggers and wanted to plunge them into him. Instead, she said, 'Thank you, Sheldon. It looks delicious. I marvel how you manage to present synthetic trash to look like vegetables.'

'I am a master of all things, Isabelle, you know that.'

Why was he irritating her so this evening? The past year had been wonderful. She worked away for five days and the weekends were to relax. And yet her nerve ends were tingling.

'Make love to me, Sheldon. Now.'

He looked up from his plate, 'But you programmed for twenty-three hundred hours.'

Isabelle wanted to scream, *'To hell with your program,'* but she pressed her lips together and looked down. 'Yes, of course, later.'

Sheldon got up and came round to stand behind her, then bent and kissed her ear lobe. 'Would you like me to reprogram. I am also feeling a strange urge, my love. We have spent more time together than was originally detailed. In fact, my feelings for you are becoming very human. Is it possible that my circuits are developing emotions?'

'Don't be ridiculous. You're an android. I know that and you know that. Serve the dessert.'

Sheldon stepped back, but there was a little moisture in his eyes, almost like tears.

It looked like strawberries, tasted like nothing.

Isabelle drained her third glass of wine. He was doing it again: folding the cloth with precision, placing the condiments together in a perfect triangle, positioning the chairs as if they had a marked spot on the floor.

'Oh, for heavens' sake, Sheldon, sit down.'

'In ten minutes, Isabelle. That is how long it will take to stack the dishes in the washer.'

She couldn't stand it any longer; her anger with him had become overwhelming. She was losing control. For fifty-one weeks they had enjoyed perfect weekends, what was wrong with her? Sheldon had seemed the solution to her life. She had a career, a thousand credits each month, a city apartment and Sheldon for relaxation.

Programmed Sheldon!

She was so deep in thought, that she didn't know he was there until his warm lips touched her neck.

'Now?'

Isabelle looked at the clock. One minute to eleven.

'No. Go away.'

'Away? Away where? To our bedroom?'

'Yes. No. Wait.'

She turned and looked at him – he was so handsome! She had been extremely selective when she marked the boxes for his features, manners and masculine attributes.

19

So why was she being so contrary? She could pick a new one next week; try out a continental gigolo, a hunk from the outback? But she didn't want to change him. That was her dilemma.

Isabelle rose and went to him. She put her arms round his neck and whispered in his ear.

Sheldon laughed against her neck, 'That is very naughty of you.'

He picked her up and went out through the door.

The March sunshine was warm as they walked beside the river. Hedgerows were showing the faintest hint of green and narcissi were breaking into flower.

'Sheldon, look, there's a nest over in the reeds.'

'Just like last year. This was our first walk together, remember?'

'Yes, I do.' And this would be the last. The thought sent her into a spiral of memories: Sheldon experiencing life with her, enjoying what she enjoyed and storing it away to remember later when they talked and laughed. She didn't want to come here again with another.

'Shall we lunch at The Duck, in the old cellar room? Reminisce about highwaymen and stagecoaches?'

'No.' The cellar was her favourite retreat, but not today. 'The Moon Room. Up-to-date. Perhaps they have a picture of the new Crater Base complex. I hear it houses a hundred-thousand people.'

Sheldon made no comment, but took her hand and raised it to his lips. 'Are you all right, Isabelle?'

'Yes, of course. Let's go and eat.'

The Moon Room was only half full, as most of the clientele preferred the old haunt downstairs.

After the meal Sheldon asked, 'Caffina or Aftersweet?'

There was reproach in Isabella's voice as she answered. 'Sheldon, you know I love the thick syrup drink. After all, you were the one who enticed me to try it. I'll have the green mint, please.'

He ordered two.

After they were served, Isabelle noticed he was fidgeting with his glass.

'You are agitated, Sheldon, do you have a circuit problem?'

He took his hand away. 'No!' His brown eyes looked into hers. 'Time is running out.'

Isabelle could see something in his gaze that she had not expected. Love, desire and pain, all rolled into one. Dynamite exploded into her, piercing her heart. 'Yes. Do you want this to end?' Sheldon did not reply. 'I'm sorry, that is not for you to say.'

'Shall we go? The light is fading and the temperature is dropping. I'll set the fire to come on.' He tapped in a code on his wristband. 'You'll be all warm and cosy, in your little antique cottage.'

Isabelle picked up her bag from beside the chair and stood up. 'You sound disapproving?'

'No. Jealous of who will come after me.'

She was shocked by his reply and realised that they were both going through a form of trauma this weekend. What did that mean? What emotional part of him was fighting the countdown, the hours they had left together? Was she jealous of who would have Sheldon next?

'Let's go home.' She didn't want to think beyond tomorrow.

Every Sunday, Sheldon brought Isabelle breakfast in bed at nine hundred hours on the dot.

It was set out to perfection on the tray, including one flower, always picked from the garden.

'Is this daffodil real?'

'Yes, but from the glasshouse. I know they are your spring favourite.'

'Old fashioned me. I do love you, Sheldon.' She stopped abruptly. 'I mean, I love your consideration, your ...'

Sheldon turned away and pressed the switch on the wall and the curtains opened to let in the morning sun.

'Another beautiful day, would you like to go for a drive?'

'Later. I thought we might edit our images before I return to the city.'

'As you wish. I will collect them and put them on the oak table.'

Isabelle sensed an indefinable tension growing between them. This made her impatient with him. 'Oh, do stop being so bloody precise. How many minutes is it going to take you – ten point three-three-three recurring? What will the never-ending fraction do to you? Send you up in smoke.'

She moved the tray and threw back the covers. 'Sheldon, I didn't mean that, I didn't mean to ... Oh! What a wicked thing to say.'

Sheldon reached for her and drew her close. But he did not deny her words.

'Get ready, Isabelle. I'll see you later.'

Isabelle waited beside Sheldon. The early evening sky was clear and the stars resembled sparkling diamonds. A humming vibration sounded, signalling the mono-train would arrive in a few seconds.

'Don't work too many late nights next week. The High Council will drain you dry if they can.'

Work was the last thing on her mind.

All Isabelle could think about was next weekend.

There would be no Sheldon to meet her, no Sheldon to comfort her and no Sheldon to share her hours with. 'I promise.'

The humming grew louder and she looked into Sheldon's eyes. It was there, again, that explosive dynamite. He pulled her close and kissed her. Then got into the car and drove off.

In her apartment, Isabelle lay awake all night.

At six hundred hours she got up and went to her desk, switched on the lamp and connected into her satellite link system. She tapped in several codes and the screen flashed the form that had been saved for the last year. Her finger hovered over the boxes that said 'retain or return'. Then she touched a box.

She picked up the phone and tapped in a number. Sheldon's voice answered.

'Sheldon, it's Isabelle. Please tap in code nine-zero-zero-nine.' She heard the pinging on his wristband, but not the final voice confirmation. 'Sheldon?'

'Are you sure? Nine-zero is to retain, but adding zero-nine will convert to all human functions. I could be late to meet you at the station; we might quarrel, fall out and not speak to each other, might ...'

'Oh, Sheldon, please just push the button. What joy! I'll be home in ...' Isabelle looked at the clock, 'three hours, fifty-five minutes and nine seconds. Just have the mattress heater turned on.'

Isabelle opened up her mail box and tapped on her group department address file, laughing as she typed:

Due to family circumstances
I shall be taking this week
as part of my annual leave

HALF A BANANA

Summer 1945

I knocked loudly on the front door. Gran's footsteps sounded and when the door opened she said, 'There's a special present for you on the table.'

I rushed into the kitchen. In my place was a yellow banana. A *real fruit* banana. Something I had seen only in books! I felt the skin and put it to my nose, sniffing the flavour. It didn't curve as much as the picture book, but I could feel the ridges.

'What do you think of it?' asked Gran, as she put my dinner before me.

'I don't know, I've never had a banana. Not one that I can remember! What does it taste like?'

'Well, it's firm to bite and... tastes lovely.'

'That doesn't tell me what it tastes like.'

'I know. You can take half back to school for afternoon play.'

'And if I like it, I'll have the other half when I come home.'

Through the classroom window, the sun was hot on my back and the brown paper bag beside me. I looked at it many times wondering what it would taste like. Would it be sharp like some of the apples I ate? Or the plums we sometimes received from Mrs Archer? What about Aunt Kate's pears that we helped pick in September? All of these had their own special taste.

Hurry up playtime.

Oh dear, the bottom of the bag is wet. What has happened to my half a banana?

The skin has gone brown and it's squashy. It won't peel! My fingers are all messy and it tastes warm and slimy. Ugh! I don't like banana.

It was five years before I tried another one.

SUMMER FLOWER

I am Summer Flower of the Cheyenne. I was born sixteen summers ago when the sun was high in the spirit world above us, and the buffalo grazed on the Great Plains.

Today the sun does not show and the daylight is short and the nights are long and cold. I have around my shoulders a fur skin, pounded and softened by the squaws and traded by my father, Running Deer, as a wedding gift to me. For when the moon shines round I will lay with my man-brave, Storm Cloud, for the first time.

It is not a good time for our ceremony. There is much discontent and the elders sit smoking their pipes and discuss much about the troubles with the White Man. I hear my mother and the other squaws say we have lost much of our land and have only a small part left. This has been called an Indian Reservation.

Three full seasons ago, what the White Man called 1861, six Cheyenne Chiefs, including our Chief Black Kettle, and four Arapaho Chiefs marked a paper called the *Treaty of Fort Wise*. It gave much of our great buffalo plains away. The Dog Soldier and other Cheyenne Chiefs who were not there have been angered by the signing. They say we were cheated, because it was not agreed by all the tribes and they will not abide by it.

There has been much fighting and death, much distrust and hatred. Now we have come to Fort Lyon with Chief Black Kettle to make peace. The fort's White Chief told Black Kettle to travel north to Sand Creek. That a White Man's flag must fly above Black Kettle's tepee, as a peace sign and we would be protected.

With the White Man's promise, my father, with the other braves, has gone hunting.

The day is ending and the sun is leaving our world. Here in our tepee, my mother lies in a deep sleep.

Soon the night demons will prowl the land, hunting for any brave that strays from the firelight.

I do not fear the dark or the demons.

Since this summer past, I have been blessed with the power of the Shaman. If he knew, I would be killed, for I am a threat to him and his honoured place beside Chief Black Kettle. I do not understand why I have been chosen – a squaw of no standing in the great Cheyenne nation. But I have, and I must go to meet the spirits; for I sense a strangeness of my mind that is calling to be answered.

I need take only my hidden sack and fur skin to keep out the cold.

There are no sounds coming from the village. Chief Black Kettle must also be asleep; his mind has retreated from the turmoil of asking the Great Spirit for guidance with the White Man. The few horses tethered to the line are also silent; it is strange, for they neigh and shuffle their hooves when the braves are here.

The tepee flap was secured tight to keep the warmth of our fire inside, but it has not stopped me leaving. I pass two rings of tepees to leave the circle of light from the fire and I am now with the darkness and the demons.

I climb the earth slope, for it will give me sight of my Cheyenne people asleep and safe. Why does the thought *safe* trouble me? We have the White Chief's flag of promise. Perhaps it is because all our fighting braves are away – only the old and young ones remain and they have but the strength of a squaw – useless against an enemy. I must not dwell on this, my spirit calls and I must light a fire with the wood I have stored here.

Now the fire burns bright and the smoke is rising in the cold air. It is not yet time for the white covering to come and keep us in our tepees. This winter I shall be warm against Storm Cloud, hoping that our seeds have met and come the next summer, I shall bring our papoose into the tribe.

I have made a feather head-dress and a wolf mask to wear. I know that the she-wolf is to be my spirit. She came to me in my sleep, out of the white light, grey in colour and with teeth that showed yellow when she snarled and snapped at the birds I killed in my dream. I am putting them on now – there is a smell from the skin I used – but the spirit and I must be as one.

I have watched the Shaman when he has been searching for his spirit – he dances round the fire and calls with strange words for answers. I must do the same.

The smoke is thickening – now is the time.

It is cold, but without wind. I drop the fur from my shoulders and begin to dance. Now I must scatter the dried roots and berries from my pouch into the fire to release their strong scent that will pass into my mind and let my spirit roam free. I imitate the Shaman – shuffle my feet in half-steps, hunch my shoulders and dip my wolf-head and raise it to look into the smoke.

There is nothing there, only the drifting column stretching towards the blackness of the spirit world. There is something missing – I must chant words to call my spirit. Had I sung in my dream? I close my eyes and the words come – rhythmic and low. I circle my fire and chant.

My mind is drifting, searching for the she-wolf. I see her coming out of the light and out of my mind. I open my eyes and she is there, circling in the column of smoke.

'Spirit, tell me what you know? Tell me why I have this fear for my people?'

The she-wolf circles higher and leaps from the fire and stands before me. She raises her head and howls a silent cry, then turns and runs with speed away across the plain, towards Fort Lyon.

I do not know the ways of the Shaman after he has released his spirit. But I feel spent and tired, my mind confused. The white light has gone and in its place is blackness that is devouring me – mind, body and soul – I cannot fight it but must give in to its demand.

I have come through into the light.

I can see the she-wolf. She is waiting by the fire, her tongue lolling and her sides heaving. She has run far and fast. I am cold although the fire still burns. Where is my fur? I need it on or I shall perish like a flower cupped in the hands of an autumn frost.

I sit by the fire and the warmth is good.

The flames are turning red and my spirit wolf returns to the smoke and disappears.

The pale light of dawn is creeping through my village and it is as silent as when I left in the dark – no one is awake. The smoke is turning blue and I can see blue-coated soldiers swaying with the firewater that makes them wild and dangerous. A White Chief is amongst them. He is waving his arms, directing them into lines. They are undisciplined. Those on foot are loading their fire-sticks; those on horse are waving their long knives; they are all facing my village.

Great open-mouthed guns spit out balls of death.

My heart and head are beating with the rhythm of a drum.

The White Chief is pointing with his long knife and the blue-coats are firing and moving forward. They are firing on our tepees – but we have their flag flying! It is our protection.

The soldiers are not stopping. They are now at the outer tepees – they are using the short knives on their fire-sticks to stab the women coming out. The horsemen are galloping forward, slashing and stabbing the old braves, who are trying to defend with their tomahawks – but they are overwhelmed by the blue soldiers.

The village is a battle place. My people are being killed.

In the smoke the squaws and children are screaming, silent open mouthed screams as they run before the soldiers who are cutting them with their long knives – a baby is torn from its mother's arms and the knife pierces its tiny body, then she is slain.

The fire is turning yellow.

The blue-coats are burning the tepees. The young are crawling out, terrified without the braves and warriors to defend them. They are chased and caught. The soldiers are frothing from the mouth, eyes wild with lust. They slice the manhood of the children and defile the young squaws before the eyes of their mothers.

The smoke is changing to grey.

Chief Black Kettle is raising a white flag, the totem of surrender, but it is being ignored. Our chief is running – running with the old and children. All are fleeing from death. The soldiers are burning every tepee – our only shelter from the winter storms.

I cannot bear to look any longer. My eyes have been filled with the horror. My head pounds, my limbs shake and my tongue is swelling with thirst. To which spirit should I plead for this wickedness not to happen? Has the Shaman seen the same? I curse this power I have been given – that I must sit here and know this is to come. That I am not able to change what has been shown to me.

It is to be.

The fire is dying to ash.

My heart is torn into fragments, each piece crying for a dead soul who will lie on the cold earth. My pain is so great that I fear my body cannot cradle and hold so many dead. Yet I have been chosen to see this and to survive.

Why?

The smoke is returning.

The she-wolf spirit has not finished. Shimmering into being is Storm Cloud and I am beside him with a papoose.

Now I see my son-brave. He is not dressed like us, he is in the cloth of the White Man: long coat and trousers; a shirt. His long hair is tied like a horse's tail and he is holding a round hard head-dress. He stands before a White Man's building the size of a mountain.

Is this why I have been chosen? Am I part of the future, my son a leader of our people in the White Man's world?

The she-wolf is looking at me, her eyes locked on mine. She is beautiful, my spirit. She has left me with the answer to my fear – my people are to be massacred here at Sand Creek at dawn.

WINGED COFFIN

A wooden coffin, six feet long, twelve inches wide and fifteen inches deep, was strapped onto the roof rack of a car that sped southwards through the Kent countryside.

At the Dover ferry, no one questioned who was in the coffin. The stevedore signalled the car into its parking place and moved on. It could have been granny getting a free ride.

The French Customs men smiled, waved the car on; they found nothing unusual to see a coffin on a car. There could be a stash of diamonds inside, but what did they care? It would mean lots of form filling and sign language. It was easier to let it pass.

Weaving through the busy town, then between fields of wheat and maize, the car and coffin diminished into a dot through the avenue of trees.

The Belgians were as nonchalant as the Frenchmen. A nod at the blue passports, and we were onwards to Liege, and, Ladies of the Night. What if there had been bags of coke winging by?

A whiz through Luxembourg and then…

Oh! Here comes the German border. Now there would be an inquisition. Up went the hand – stop. Another cursory look at Her Majesty's Coat of Arms, a curt nod and off went the car and coffin into Deutschland. It motored beside the Moselle vineyards, alongside the Rhine and over hills that grew into mountains.

The Swiss border had a road barrier and the Customs men spoke English. Now the coffin would be opened. What was that? They only wanted to know if the car had a motorway licence. Of course it did! Find it, someone, and stick it on the windscreen. The barrier was lifted and the car, with brass handles knocking against the coffin ends, passed through. They didn't care if the missing Great Train Robbery loot was inside, more pennies for the bankers.

In the land of mountains, valleys and lakes the journey ended. On a plateau above a village, in a pasture of wild flowers, lay the coffin. The lid was lifted. The mystery revealed.

What were you expecting, a pagan ritual burial?

Sorry, just the holiday playthings – hubby's model glider and the kid's kites!

Where is it now? Tied to the garage rafters; six feet 'above' the ground.

PHOBIA

The only splash of colour on the pale corridor walls were framed prints of the countryside and evenly spaced teak wood doors, each with a single nameplate.

Behind one of these, the sun shone through a high barred window onto a man sitting in a legless, rounded upholstered chair; his thin frame bent beneath hunched shoulders.

The hiss of the hydraulic door made him look up and he registered his surroundings: in the ceiling a single, round opaque light that was never turned off, and cream-cloth walls buttoned at intervals. His eyes searched for the hidden door and, as it opened, a broad figure in a blue striped dress entered carrying a tray.

The man drew his legs up under his chin and hugged them with long-boned fingers. He dropped his head so that he didn't have to look at the giant ant walking towards him, with its smiling black face, spiked dark hair and large eyes.

It spoke, 'Medicine time, John.'

The hypodermic needle pricked his skin and black claws pushed the plunger down and then caressed the hole in his arm with a swab.

A black-jointed hairy arm encircled his shoulders, cradled him into its soft belly and a claw brushed the thin grey hair from his forehead.

He struggled to free himself from its suffocating warmth, leapt from the chair and scrambled under the plastic framed bed. The door hissed open and closed. He was safe again.

The ants had started annoying him when they were babies, their little black bodies scurried back and forth from a crack in the concrete outside his back door. They marched in rows through the flowerbeds, circled under the shed, in and out of the rock plants hunting for food. They had grown bigger. They climbed the shed door and disappeared inside, stealing minute pieces of wood shaving. He had swept them off with a broom, sprinkled killer powder, even burnt them, but still they marched, day after day after day.

They got bolder; the military lines came over the doorstep along the hall skirting into the kitchen. They grew fatter and fatter on his jam and sugar; stronger, so that he couldn't push them away. And they grew even bigger. They crawled up the stairs, into his bed. They wanted him. They wanted his flesh, his eyes and his brain. He had tried to fight them off. Finally, he ran into the street, but they clung to him, clawed him down into the gutter. Frantic with fear he had cried out for help.

It was the postman who saved him; wiped them away.

But one had followed him here; the one who came in, bloated with food, and jabbed him with poisonous needles.

A regular pattern of daylight followed by darkness passed the barred window.

He heard the hiss of the door.

Fear ran through him like a torrent of water breaking a dam; a pain started in his chest, he felt hot and his mouth went dry.

The mutated ant came towards him pushing a wheelchair. The legs and arms had become human and as it helped him from his chair, he noticed it had fingers with creamy nails. Ant-woman still grinned and spoke soothingly, hypnotically. 'Don't be afraid, John, we are going for a little ride to say 'hello' to the other patients.'

They went along a corridor and swing doors opened. Ants of all sizes turned to look at him. They were all here; they had come from his garden to claim him. He twisted in the wheelchair, raised both hands to cover his eyes. His mouth opened and closed, but no words came out, although his mind screeched, No! You can't have me.

'Come, John, turn round and let me introduce you. They are harmless – believe me.'

He squirmed and dribble ran down his chin. Lowering his hands, he opened his eyes. He saw people. Human people, knitting, reading, playing cards – ordinary people – but he was still afraid. She wheeled him amongst them; one touched him, placed her warm hands over his cold ones, but he was glad when he was taken back to his silent, safe room.

It had been a trick; they were coming for him out of the walls. First the one with the clicking needles, then the card player, its fan of cards like a barbed spearhead. He flung himself against the wall, hitting out with bunched fists, head-butting them between the eyes. He kicked at their legs until they faded back into the padded cloth. He had fought his demons with body and mind and was victorious. He would not let them invade his life again.

The door hissed. The ant-woman had gone and Sadie had taken its place. 'Good afternoon, John. How are you today?'

His wall of silence stood firm as he watched the dark skinned nurse with large, red-framed spectacles walk towards him. Had he been so ill that he thought her an ant? Foolish man! Yet, he couldn't speak to her; it was as though his voice box had seized up, like a broken motor-engine.

'It's time to see your Doctor. Will you walk and then visit the Lounge on the way back?' He nodded. 'Fine, off we go.'

The weeks of care showed. He straightened his shoulders and got out of the chair. Flesh had thickened over the thin frame and he linked his arm through Sadie's as they walked out into the corridor.

He moved to a new room with green walls and a carpeted floor; although it still had a barred window. He felt trusted because they didn't lock the door and he could walk along the corridor to the Lounge. He didn't see them now as ants; but as human puppets without strings. Like the skeletal man in striped pyjamas, who moved slowly and shuffling, always with a blanket round his shoulders, a mimic of an emaciated prisoner of war, while another man jumped around like a sprung pogo stick. He never spoke to anyone, just sat and watched.

His final step towards recovery was when he walked from the confines of the hospital into the garden. A breeze lifted his hair, rippled across his face and his eyes watered with joy. Across the lawn were oval flowerbeds of Busy Lizzies and dahlias, and a perfume was carried from the rose arbour. Gardening was his hobby, more than that, his life's pleasure – until the ants had appeared. Were they here? He began poking his finger around the plants; he couldn't see any. Good, this gardener had them beaten. Tense and wary he sat with Sadie on a bench and cried.

His bed was made and the room was bare except for a small holdall packed ready for his return home. Strange feelings were stirring in the pit of his stomach, his heartbeat quickened as thoughts of the outside world crowded in, but he fought to hold them down. Everything would be all right; he was in control.

Sadie walked with him to the taxi; patted his hand as she said goodbye.

In the sunshine his front garden looked neat and tidy. The hallway smelt fresh, the kitchen spotless, every shelf washed clean with new pots of jam. He went upstairs and stopped at the closed bedroom door, his hand shook as he reached for the handle. Someone had been busy on his behalf; there wasn't even a dirty sock to be seen.

Back in the kitchen he plugged in the kettle then opened the backdoor – and froze.

They were there, waiting for him. He had told that hook-nosed doctor, over and over, the ants were after him, *only him*. Panic made him go dizzy and his hands tingled with pins and needles. He sank down onto the floor as they marched over the doorstep towards him.

The shrill of the doorbell penetrated his senses, but his body felt like stone, too heavy to move. It shrilled again, this time longer. He rolled onto his side and crawled to the newel post at the bottom of the stairs and pulled himself up. Again the bell, this time it rang continuously.

He reached the door and fumbled with the latch and Sadie came in.

'*What's wrong*, John?'

His stricken stare told all. Mute, he moved to the backdoor and pointed. They were not there, just the late summer sunshine on the brightly coloured flowerbeds.

MYRMECOPHOBIA - Fear of ants

MAD, MAD HUSBAND

Who in their right mind, would canoe under the town of Reading? Well, my husband, Tony, and his canoe partner, Bob, did just that!

They were practising for the 125-mile Easter weekend Devizes to Westminster Canoe Race. It is an annual event that uses the Kennet and Avon Canal, the River Thames and the tidal reach from Teddington to the finish at Westminster Bridge.

One Sunday morning they had planned a practice run down the Thames.

Imagine – a twenty-two inches wide racing K2 canoe, twenty-two foot long, with two young men leaning into their strokes skimming downstream from Caversham

Lock. The decision to change course into the Kennet Canal and portage Blakes Lock, then paddle on pass the Abbey ruins and Reading Prison was never explained.

Why deviate, you wonder? Might practising get a bit boring? Perhaps they wanted a change of scenery?

At the west-end of the backwater, the Holybrook emerges. This is the stream that used to bring water to the monks of Reading Abbey.

Curiosity led them *upstream*, until they came to a tunnel, about ten feet wide and high enough to enter.

Only mad-cap youth would dare venture inside.

They didn't even have a torch.

Picture their journey:

Light fading from behind; darkness ahead. The only sound, running water, as they dip their paddles into the stream. Feel the air chill and touch the wet brick walls, slimy with algae. Hear the scratching of rats and wonder what creepy-crawlies are running over your damp t-shirt. Blackness, that blots out everything. Their echoing words eerie, disembodied.

Paddle under the Kings Road junction at Jacksons Corner. Dim light, like a barred prison window shafts through a drain.

Under the 200-year-old cobbled courtyard of the George Hotel. Where long ago travellers rested and ate, whilst the stablemen changed the stagecoach horses journeying on to London.

Suddenly, ahead, a circle of daylight, the tunnel ends.

Paddle past the hotel kitchen window and a surprised modern day chef.

In a few seconds, paddle back into the dark tunnel. Dipping paddles under the Post Office Telephone Exchange, then into daylight at Minster Street.

The Holybrook swings left, going underground again. Flows on like a snake under Simonds Brewery at Bridge Street. Under its great beer vats and cobbled yard. Their paddles force the canoe on, under Fobney Street and past County Lock.

On through the darkness, dripping walls, in places the paddle blades touching the silted bottom. The only daylight filtering through the occasional drain-grille and badly fitting manhole covers.

Then, after an adventure of no more than a mile, they paddle out into sunlight at Brook Street.

Shouts of 'We did it!', and journeys end.

I hope at that moment of victory they questioned the recklessness of their adventure. Thoughts such as: how do you turn a twenty-two foot canoe in a ten foot wide tunnel or get unstuck when the roof lowered and they had to use their shoulders? Youth the explorer rarely considers such things. And the sight of a racing canoe being carried, at a run, through Reading on a Sunday morning in 1974 was less of an oddity than it might be today.

My reaction when they arrived home? 'Oh. You paddled under Reading? How nice. Lunch is nearly ready.'

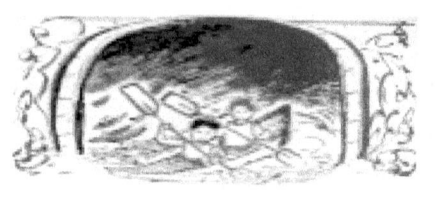

LOVE IS...

Nina Loukas dropped her silk wrap on the bed. Naked and bronzed she picked up a jar of cream, scooped the expensive jelly on to her fingers and spread it over her belly. There were still a few stretch lines she'd like to erase. She posed with her hands high above her head and looked at her reflection in the mirror. Pregnancy had not changed her; she was still beautiful, tall, dark haired and sensual – the mistress of Hektor Panos, one of Athens' richest men.

Nina slipped the wrap back on. She was going to pamper herself today with a massage, a new hair style and if she had time, a new dress from one of her favourite boutiques.

A cry from her son made her hurry through the connecting door into the nursery. She gently picked him up and laid him over her shoulder.

'There, there, my sweet. Mama is here.' Nina rocked her son until he settled. After she laid him down, she stroked her finger over his head, a frown creasing her forehead. The landing door opened and his day nurse came in shaking a bottle of formula milk.

'Eron's still fretful, Maria. I'll be back by four, any problems phone me.'

'I will, Nina. Have a nice day.' This cliché always irritated, but the girl was a gem and she said nothing to upset her.

Thirty minutes later she drove out of the underground garage of her Chelsea apartment.

Nina relaxed as the masseur's hands stroked her back. Lying face down after so many months was wonderful and she was enjoying every moment as his fingers circled and kneaded her shoulders.

'Fedor, I think a few more minutes and then a steam bath. Will you ask Rosa to make sure she is free for my facial afterwards?'

'Of course, Miss Loukas, I will go as soon as we are finished. We've missed your visits over the last few months. May I ask how your little son is faring?'

'Eron is the most beautiful baby ever born and will grow to be the most handsome man in the whole of Europe. How can he be otherwise when he has *two* Grecian parents?'

She hadn't seen Hektor for two weeks; he was in Geneva negotiating a deal with old Altair Kairis, but he was back this afternoon. Everything she was doing today was for Hektor tonight.

She felt a little tap on her bottom. 'All finished, Miss Loukas. I would suggest at least three times next week, to get you toned back into shape.'

'You make it sound as if I've gone to flab, Fedor. My little Eron was not a large baby, my Mama was most disappointed.'

'Never,' Fedor bowed to her, 'you are a Greek goddess, Miss Loukas, forever.'

'Flattery will get you a large gratuity. Ask Reception to add twenty percent to my account.' Nina wrapped a large white towel around her and clipped the opening with a butterfly clasp. Fedor opened the door and she walked down the corridor to the steam room.

Knightsbridge was teeming with tourists, all rushing to get their Harrods green bags, even if it only held a bar of chocolate. Nina turned into a narrow street and then through an unobtrusive varnished door. She went up the stairs to the first floor and into a salon adorned with pale silk wall hangings and matching velvet settees. Sitting behind a Georgian table was a petite woman, her dark hair coiffured in a smooth chignon; her blood red fingernails making a dramatic contrast against a black dress.

'Nina, *ma chère*, at last you are here for something other than the *robe de grossesse.*'

'Oh, Francine, yes, they are gone. I want something flimsy, feminine, low cut and rose pink. I am going to seduce Hektor tonight, all night; we will not sleep until the dawn.' Nina laughed, 'Shame on me, *Madame*, but I am Greek and you are French. We can admit all. Yes?'

'*Oui, Mademoiselle*. Come and sit down, I will bring you the *robe extraordinaire.*'

A young assistant removed Nina's coat. '*Merci*, Minna,' and she sat on one of the settees. Nina chose four gowns to try on. Each one was beautiful, but the last was what she'd been dreaming about for the last six months. 'I'll take this one with me now, Francine. Will you have a new wardrobe ready for me to view next week?'

'Of course, I will phone when it is ready. This season's colours and styles are perfect for you.'

Nina nodded, 'Thank you, *au revoir.*'

She hurried out into the street, feeling young again, refreshed in body and soul, yet all she wanted was to go home and hold her son.

*

The spring day had turned into a starlit evening. Nina closed the curtains and dimmed the lights. An orange glow from the fire reflected off the scallop shells decorating the walls, giving the room a touch of Grecian magic and warmth.

She straightened a napkin on the small round table, adjusted Hektor's silver knife to match her own. Everything was perfect. She turned and looked in the large scroll-framed mirror: the rose pink dress was a deception of beauty, its line hiding the little extra plumpness she still had around her hips. Tonight she'd left her girdle hidden away in the dressing room. There was to be nothing to hinder Hektor's caresses when he arrived.

She opened the nursery door and tiptoed across to Eron's cradle. She had bathed and clothed him in a new white sleeping suit, the scent of his baby talc fresh and wholesome. He was so perfect. She had loved him from the moment of conception, through those difficult early months, and even when she walked like a waddling duck. She had thought her love could not grow any more, but the moment he was placed in her arms her heart had found the extra space for him beside her Hektor forever.

Nina heard the front door open. Her lover was here.

She smiled, and whispered, 'Sleep well and long, Eron, tonight is for your Mama and Papa.'

Hektor dropped his brief case on the floor and held out his arms. When he was away, their only contact was a few telephone calls. He never emailed, joking that secretary's eyes loved to pry given the opportunity. She went to him looking like the woman he had met at that magazine launch, three years ago. She had walked into that room and a magnetic, unrealistic desire had run through her. But she had held back. He was an icon, a celebrity, married, a father and a catholic. She could only be his mistress, a hidden love. Yet, guilt had not stopped her. Now they had a son, a second sin, but so be it.

She went into his arms, stood close so he could feel her slimness. She circled her arms around his neck and touched his lips with hers. Words were not needed as he kissed her with a hunger she understood.

'Welcome home, darling,' she whispered.

Hektor held her even tighter. 'Yes, home, my dearest.'

As they parted, he looked at her properly. 'You are perfect again. And you are wearing my favourite colour.' He ran his finger along the neckline, stopped at the bottom point and slipped his finger down between her breasts.

'It's just for you, Hektor. But, you must need a drink, was everything a success?'

'Yes. Signed, sealed and settled. I'll have a whisky after I've showered.'

Hektor went into their bedroom, but did not close the door.

She smiled and followed.

***

Nina sat in the elegant Georgian décor of the consultant's waiting room. Over the past weeks it had become a place of heartache and fear. Her hands wouldn't stop shaking as she hugged Eron tightly against her, while he, oblivious to all chanted, 'Bear, bear,' and bounced his teddy bear up and down.

The door opened. 'Dr Milos will see you now, Miss Loukas.'

Hektor was away, yet again. This time she resented his absence. He should be here. Here to help her and his son face the man who might be going to pass a dreadful sentence on their child? She stood up, Eron in her arms. Her legs didn't want to move, her heart beat so hard it felt like a pain and her mouth was so dry. But she followed the woman out and across the corridor into the doctor's room.

Dr Milos stood behind his desk. He was the image of Saville Row in his dark suit over a white shirt, a perfectly knotted red tie. There was a slight smile, but no happy greeting. 'Good morning, Miss Loukas. Please, sit down.'

Nina acknowledged with a nod, sitting in one of the green silk cushioned chairs. He didn't speak and she wrapped her arms round Eron, wanting to protect him from the doctor's grave expression.

Dr Milos walked round his desk and sat in the other chair opposite her. He touched Eron's hand with his finger. 'I do not have good news, I'm afraid.'

She stared at him, taking in his words, but her mind was like treacle.

'Your son is now over a year old and the tests confirm our fears. I'll not prolong my diagnosis, he has Achondroplasia, dwarfism of the arms and legs and ...' he paused, 'I am very sorry.'

Sorry! He was sorry! Her perfect baby was going to be deformed, ridiculed. She couldn't think! Where was Hektor when she needed him most? Did money mean more to him than their son? In that moment she hated him. He had abandoned her. Had he suspected this result? Had he found out and left her to face this alone?

Eron wriggled and she looked down. She stroked his dark baby curls that she hadn't cut yet. Maybe the tests were wrong? Maybe they had got muddled up and belonged to someone else? How could this be true? Hektor and she were so normal, so perfect to look at.

'This is not what any parent wants to hear, but there is help and advice available. I have a package of information for you. But, of course, please ask me anything you wish to know.'

All Nina could think was why? Why my son?

'Is there a cure, any treatment? Money is not a problem. Please, I can take him anywhere, anywhere in the world.' Hektor could pay. He always paid.

'I won't give you false hope, Miss Loukas. There is no cure. Money cannot buy it for him. At worst he could be only three foot tall, at best five foot and his head will be disproportionately large. I feel it best you understand this now.'

Nina's whole world was crumbling with each word the consultant uttered. She ought to say something, ask lots of questions, but what? Her mind was blank, an empty hole of nothing.

His professional manner softened. 'Would you like to go with my secretary and have a moment to yourself? She will make you a cup of coffee. Nurse James will look after Eron.'

'Thank you. Yes. I need time ... I need to think, speak to Eron's father.' She got up, lifting Eron on to her arm, conscious how small he was for his age. A lump filled her throat, she loved him so much. Had she loved him too much? Was this her punishment for conceiving him out of wedlock? Had God done this? Her whole body was a bag of trembling terror. The throbbing tick in her temple was getting worse.

The door opened and his secretary came in. Nina let the woman guide her towards the door and Dr Milos' voice followed her out. 'I would like to see Eron next month;

then we can decide on a way forward –' any other words were cut off as the door closed.

The coffee was hot and strong. Nina wrapped her cold hands round the fine china mug and hugged it until her mind cleared. The family life she had imagined with Hektor and Eron would now take an alternative path yet with the same outcome. Eron would achieve his goals and take his place in society, maybe with a stronger personality than any man standing beside him. She looked across at the young nurse playing with him and his teddy bear. Tears slipped down her cheeks. She would do anything to spare him the years to come, but she couldn't, all she could do was teach him how to live.

'Thank you for the coffee, Mrs Wilson. I want to go home now, Eron needs his lunch.'

'Of course you do dear. I've made your next appointment for four weeks today.' She handed Nina a printed card and a sealed package. 'Would you like me to order you a taxi?'

'Yes, please. Thank you Vicki for playing with Eron.'

'It was a pleasure, Miss Loukas. Goodbye, Eron, see you soon.'

Nina picked up her son and left the building. In the taxi each time she thought of Hektor her anger grew. She had no idea where he was – his call last week was from Dubai. She would have to phone the hotel there and see if they knew where he was going on to. He would be furious if she contacted his London office, but she had to speak to him, *now!*

Hektor came to the apartment two days later.

They sat on the settee facing each other. Nina gazed at his perfect body, long limbs and the dark wavy hair. His handsome face was tanned and those grey eyes that could show such love for her were full of tears.

'Oh, darling, I should have been with you. But life has been very arduous. I have lost so much money; the financial situation is still very precarious. I am holding things together, but ...' he paused, 'there is not a bottomless pit of cash anymore.'

'What do you mean?'

'Eron will need a lot of care, special equipment. There must be special schooling. I ... I might have to reduce your allowance. There is my wife and my children to consider.'

Nina lifted her head, seeing his face colour.

'I see. I am the mistress who must come second when things go wrong. Your duty remains firstly to your wife.'

'No. I did not mean that, but Nina, a dwarf child? *Fathered* by me?'

'Are you accusing me of being unfaithful?'

'I will not belittle myself with an answer.' But Hektor's face flushed crimson.

She stood up and went into the nursery and lifted Eron from his cot and took him back into the sitting room.

'Where is Maria? I should not like her listening –'

Nina raised her hand, stopping him in mid-sentence.

'She is not here; I gave her the day off. Do you think me that stupid? Tell me this is not your son. Look at him closely, while he is still a baby, before he changes too much.'

Hektor got up and embraced them together. 'I'm sorry, Nina. I don't know what I was thinking. Of course Eron is mine. But I won't be around much from now on. I have a lot of travelling to do, deals to set up and complete. But I'll try and make sure your allowance stays the same.'

But Nina knew this was the beginning of the end.

'Thank you. I think you should now leave your key on the hall table.' She felt him stiffen then kiss her temple, his tears on her cheek. But the reality remained. He was leaving.

A moment later the front door closed.

Nina couldn't believe Hektor had ended their relationship as though he were withdrawing from a business deal gone bad. Did he see Eron as a never ending burden, a threat to his family? She could have pleaded with him, but a rift had already grown between them and would widen. She had put Hektor on a pedestal like a Greek God, but he was afraid, a turncoat to his son who had his genes, regardless of how they had developed.

She sat down and Eron snuggled close, his little hands clinging to her. When would he become aware that he was different? She sat up straight; her love for Eron never falter. She would protect him always, for he had been conceived in love by a man she would never forget.

Nina tucked her legs up on the settee and cuddled Eron until he fell asleep. Standing up she carried him into the nursery and laid him in his cot. There were decisions to be made. She and Hektor had never talked about an end to their affair. She loved him, she trusted him. There was no signed contract for a single penny – he could stop it anytime. Hektor had paid for everything: the apartment, her designer clothes, the spa appointments, the Porsche car, plus a very generous allowance. Now, there would only be the allowance. She could go back to modelling, but she hadn't lost those extra inches needed to get her back on the glossy covers of fashion magazines.

She wandered into their bedroom – her bedroom now – it was all so painful. His presence was there, in the bed, the lover, the man she had thrown everything away to be with. She opened her wardrobe and took out the flowing rose-pink dress she had bought when Hektor came home after Eron was born. The folds had hidden the plumpness but underneath there had been nothing to hinder his caresses.

No, she had not lost everything; she would not have Eron if she hadn't met Hektor. She had accepted he would never seek a divorce. The path she had chosen she did willingly, without a second thought. Why didn't she feel angry? Why did she only ache with the sadness that she would never see him again.

The silent apartment was like a cloak keeping in the fear that was slowly filling her. What was she going to do? Where could she go? There was only one place where she could plan her and Eron's future. She would go home to Corfu, to her Greek roots – to her mother – to the villa hidden amongst the cypress trees in the hills. Eron would love the clear sea water, the tortoises that lived in the sand dunes.

Nina held the dress against her and gazed at her reflection in the mirror. She was pale now, a very different woman than what she had been a year ago. When she had worn this dress on that magical night she had been radiant with her hair swept high and held in place with an emerald clip, the colour of her eyes.

Hektor was Eron's father and he had been her husband in all the duties required of him. She needed no marriage certificate. She loved Hektor and would have been faithful to him until the day she died.

Her gaze burned into her image and the base animal instinct of a lioness surged through her and she whispered, 'I will love and protect you, Eron, always.'

SILENT NIGHT

It's Christmas Eve.

I love this night. It is full of anticipation of the pleasures to come, and these start with the song, 'As we climb the stairs...' The ceremony of hanging the stockings on the bed-rails, the numerous 'Good night, but I'm not tired,' and the final 'Father Christmas won't come if you're not asleep.'

In the kitchen the cupboard is full of naughty calories and the fridge is bulging with party goodies, turkey and ham.

My floured fingers knead the pastry trimmings and the smell of mince pies wafts from the oven.

Upstairs, the excited voices stop.

The house has become quiet, like the eye of a storm.

From the garage, two special presents take pride of place in front of the Christmas tree, a doll's house and a skateboard.

In the flickering firelight the room mellows and the tree lights enhance the colourful wrappings.

Christmas carols fill the air.

This is a time for us.

In the quietness, we toast, 'Peace and goodwill, Happy Christmas.'

GELID WORLD

Witnessed only by the billions of stars in the galaxy, an explosion of opposing gases rippled shock waves across time and tilted a minor sun a few degrees and Earth's weather was changed forever.

* * *

The Blue Sun rose like an iced diamond in the northern sky. Its cold light fell on a stream. Silver fishes flashed between green fronds and danced with the current. Gradually everything slowed and changed from a watery paradise to frozen glass.

Birds took flight, seeking shelter in hollows, eaves or barns. Grasses, autumn foliage and the brown bark of the trees – whitened.

A farm lay as if in death. No creature could be seen and the shapes of barns and fences were like artists' outlines. In the lowland, fields no longer ripened with the seasons. They were enclosed under artificial screens that were stiffening in the northerly breeze.

Painted on this whiteness, the farmhouse smoke swirled from the chimney and its windows were shuttered. The grey brick was coated with a clear film, its purpose to trap the heat within. But nothing could stop the ice covering the house.

A frozen world locked in a time capsule for the next ten days.

Shelly Collins groped for the alarm stopper; then slid her dark head back under the duvet. She ran her hand over the empty half of the bed, missing Rick's strong warm body. His promotion was great. She just didn't like him being away at Control HQ.

Images of recent years came to mind. The twenty-first century may have come in with flamboyant celebrations, but had drowned in worldwide mayhem twenty years later. Shelly had lived through a world catastrophe. Technology was useless. Ten out of every ninety days the Blue Sun dominated the world's weather.

Throwing back the cover she groaned, 'Staying tucked up warm and snug isn't getting today's work done.'

Stripes, the ginger cat, stretched in his basket when Shelly went into the kitchen.

'Hi, lazy bones, breakfast?'

Both fed and satisfied, Shelly pulled on her Ranger thermal jump-suit, rider clothes and crash helmet.

'Bye, ginger, see you tonight.'

Then she went out, locking the door of Bayford Lodge - now known as Freeze Station Alpha Seven.

Ten minutes later, the snow-scooter was a red slash across the white face of the hillside. Far below, in the valley, a wide meandering river had become a slippery grey snake. The muted colours of the weeds would disappear as the ice thickened in the days to come.

Shelly made several calls to remote farms and by mid-afternoon she reached Primrose Cottage, which looked as though a fairy had put a spell on it. Hanging from the roof, drips of rain had turned into glass needles and creeping ice made the leaded windows look cracked. Crimson, yellow and bronze dahlias were taking on white coats.

In answer to her knock, she heard feet shuffling down the corridor. Several bolts slid back and Dora Cottrell's wrinkled face peeped through a crack. Pale blue eyes brightened and the door swung open.

'Sergeant Collins. Come in, my girl.'

Taking off her helmet Shelly brushed flaked ice from her jacket.

'They've given you a new uniform?' Dora asked, as Shelly sat down at the kitchen table.

'Yes. Improved insulation, for the days when I'm out and about in these sub-zero temperatures. New badge too: Freeze Ranger.'

Dora placed a steaming mug of coffee in front of Shelly and then settled into a chair.

'I like the red colour, matches your snow-scooter. Very fashionable.'

'Thanks.'

'How are things in the big wide world?'

'Fair to middling. I would never have wished this upon us, but it has brought about a global union. That would never have happened otherwise.' Shelly sipped her coffee. 'There's talk of a Global Committee. Who knows, it may work?'

'Pigs might fly and elephants born pink, but I'll keep my fingers crossed.' Dora pulled a thick woollen cardigan from a stool and put it on. 'The temperature's starting to go down.'

When Shelly left Dora's the afternoon light was fading.

She rode into Maddock Valley and felt dwarfed by the high cliffs that stood like white marble walls, the grey crevices dark windows. Nearer the valley floor smaller rocks resembled steps. The air temperature was colder here and snowflakes started to fall. Then the wind strengthened and it turned into a blinding snowstorm. The single-track road became a ribbon of ice. The rear of the scooter was set up as a half-track, but this didn't stop the front wheels skidding and although Shelly fought the slide, it veered off the road. Body and machine parted company.

Shelly fell onto the rocks. Jagged points pierced her side and shoulder. Her helmet smashed against the rear track as the scooter flew past her on a collision course with the ground.

She lay motionless, senses stunned; it was the searing pain that kept her conscious.

As she moved, a cry left her lips, 'Bloody hell! Think! Breathe slowly … phone … scooter.' She found voicing her needs helped control the pain. 'It's getting dark … shelter.' Rolling onto her uninjured side, Shelly pulled herself up against a boulder. Her legs worked and one arm. But her left side felt on fire.

The snow-scooter had ended on its side. It looked OK, but looks could be deceiving.

Five minutes later, Shelly knew she was in trouble.

The petrol tank had fractured and the snow was soaking up the life-saving liquid.

Her Global Tracking System was in her left inside pocket, but she knew, before her fingers lifted it out, that it was broken.

She now had three priorities – shelter, warmth and help.

Her last report into Area Seven HQ had indicated that she was on her homeward run.

On an impulse, she had turned off into Maddock Pass to call on Harry Stubbs. He had fallen and broken his pelvis during the Summer Freeze Time. Orders emphasised that straying from the reported route was dangerous.

It was almost dark and the snowstorm had worsened. Flakes built in layers on her uniform and the cold was biting through into her flesh. She needed to find shelter, *now!* Taking the survival backpack from the scooter she found the weight was unbearable on her shoulder. She would have to carry it round her waist.

The howling wind and snow forced her to bend almost double to shield her visor and each step could cause her to slip and maybe break an ankle. If she fell she wouldn't be able to get up. Pain spread from her shoulder across her chest, making it difficult to breath. 'How much further?' she shouted. Then the cliff face towered out of the storm.

Shelly ran her gloved fingers along the white surface wanting to kiss the cold stone and, under the lee of the cliff, the wind was less fierce. She started to search for a crevice large enough for her, and the sleeping bag she needed to survive the night. Relief surged as she felt an opening. Bitter disappointment as her fingers penetrated just a few inches.

Her eyes flooded with tears and she blinked several times to stop them rolling down her face. The cold and pain were sapping her strength and Shelly dug deep into her mental reserves to carry on along the cliff.

Minutes seemed like hours. Then Shelly felt the opening to a cave – it was big enough for her to get in. Huddled on the ground and with her good hand she pulled the sleeping bag into shape and crawled between the warm fibres. There was a dent in her helmet, but it would be unwise to take it off. If there were a cut and blood underneath, it would have to soak into her short curls. The insulation began to warm her and she closed her eyes, then they snapped open. 'You mustn't go to sleep.' She repeated this over and over as the hours ticked by to the dawn.

Rick Collins flipped his mobile off. He looked at his watch for the tenth time in the last half-hour. Where the hell was Shelly? His wife might be the most independent, I-can-look-after-myself woman, but it was almost midnight. This was the first day of Freeze Time. There should be no emergencies yet.

Rick went into the Control HQ Ops Room and Sergeant Wilkins turned from the display screen. 'Bob, I need to contact Shelly's control unit. Can I use your set?'

'Be my guest. Trouble?'

'There's no reply from home. I need to know what's going on.'

Rick sat down and dialled up Area Seven. After a few minutes his face tightened and he asked, 'You received no sign-off call? It's gone midnight, George, something has happened.'

Bob Wilkins listened to the one sided conversation: Shelly was missing ... no SOS received ... unable to search until daylight.

'You'll let me know the minute you hear from her? Thanks.' Rick ended the transmission.

Bob spoke, 'Shelly's a bright girl; she would have got in touch if anything was wrong.'

Rick sat silent. His mind wouldn't work. He couldn't think what to do, where to go. All he could picture were mountains covered in ice, roads and tracks deadly skid pans and a red snow-scooter scattered in pieces. Shelly lying injured, maybe dead.

In the cave, Shelly watched the dark turn to dawn.

Now was the time to switch on her Personal Locator Beacon, but she needed to be outside for the rescue satellite to pick up her signal.

The minute she moved every muscle in her body exploded with pain. Beads of perspiration soaked her forehead and body heat misted her visor. She was suffocating. Wrenching the facemask up, she breathed in ice cold air. This took her breath away and another searing pain shot across her chest. Shelly controlled her panic by inhaling slowly.

Standing was impossible. Her left side had stiffened, preventing any movement, so she crawled, using her other side. Reaching the cave entrance, the Blue Sun mocked her as it rose for the second morning to increase the cold temperature on Earth.

Hanging the beacon round her neck, Shelly activated the signal. The sleepless hours caught up with her and her head dropped forward and she dozed.

Shelly woke when the first pebble hit her helmet, then a stone, then several, then a bombardment of rock crashed down around her. She screamed, 'No! Not now!' She dragged her injured body back into the cave and watched with horror as the opening was blocked with falling rocks.

Groping in the darkness, she found her survival pack, then the torch. The roof sloped from the opening down to nothing. A wedge of stone pitted with holes, like Gruyere cheese. The simile reminded her she was hungry. The pack had emergency food, water and a small stove. She needed a hot drink. Lighting the stove proved difficult one-handed, but she managed to make hot soup.

Zipped back in the sleeping bag, Shelly tried to be positive and talked to herself. It seemed to focus her mind. 'Yes, I was outside long enough for my signal to be received by HQ. They will find my scooter – know I can't be far away.'

Time passed. How long she didn't know, her watch was broken.

Ice began to whiten her sleeping bag. Coolness crept over her skin and puffs of mist left her mouth as she breathed out. She had felt panic yesterday outside in the valley, now, trapped behind the rock fall, this cave could be her tomb.

'Rick, come for me, *please*. Don't leave me here to die.'

At Control HQ, rescue boss Tom Shepherd, was prepared and ready to leave as soon as it was light. He was a big, muscular man, with white wavy hair, in his mid-fifties. He had climbed and walked the mountain ranges since a boy. All he needed for a quick and successful retrieval was Shelly's signal.

'We've got her on satellite,' Bob shouted from the Ops Room.

Hearing the shout, Rick looked up from the rucksack he was packing.

They had her. Thank God.

He waited for the co-ordinates to be marked on the map.

An hour later, two rescue vehicles entered Maddock Pass.

A leaden sky blocked out the Blue Sun and the dull whiteness of the valley sent a shudder down Rick's spine. Conditions were bad, considering it was only the second freeze day.

'Maybe we should have used a helicopter, Tom.'

'Yeh, progress is slow, but we're nearly there, another couple of miles.'

The red snow-scooter was hard to spot after the snowstorm. Even the shape had taken on a rock formation.

'Stop! Over there, on its side, her scooter.'

Rick was out of the cabin before the snowmobile came to a halt.

Red-suited Rangers fanned out across the frozen rocks, searching to and fro, like worker ants.

Shelly was nowhere to be found.

Tom called HQ. 'Can you re-affirm the co-ordinates? Over.'

'Signal ceased. It has not restarted. Over.'

Rick snatched the handset. 'You *must have it*, those batteries last over twenty-four hours.'

Tom took the handset back. 'Rick, calm down, there must be a reason for the signal to stop. Call the team back for a new briefing.'

*

Beyond the circle of torchlight, the cavern walls oozed coldness from their stone pores.

Shelly's breathing became laboured as the oxygen decreased. She fought the urge to close her eyes, knowing that if she did, it would be her final sleep.

Since the rock fall there had been scuttling noises and her four-legged companion ran up her sleeping bag. 'How are you, Ratty? Warmer than me I'm sure.' A nose and whiskers explored her visor; then it settled between her feet.

Into the silence came a faint scraping sound, growing louder with each precious breath.

Was it rescue or another rock fall?

Shelly closed her eyes. She knew if it was not rescue, her life was ended.

Outside, Rick heaved away the rocks. They were still grey, which meant the fall had been recent. He wouldn't let his mind accept that Shelly was crushed under them.

'Tom, an opening, there *is* a cave.'

Rick frantically strained at the heavy rocks, but he made an opening. His gloves ripped through to the flesh.

He crawled in and stopped. A yellow glow picked out the still body.

He cried out, 'No! We're too late!'

He lifted Shelly's shoulders and a groan passed her lips, then she opened her eyes and looked at him.

'I knew you would come for me.' With these words Shelly slipped into unconsciousness.

Later that day, Rick marched along the hospital corridor, chocolates in one hand and flowers in the other. He had his speech prepared – reckless, stupid, dangerous behaviour. It was time she gave up policing and started pushing a pram.

All this flew out the window when Rick saw Shelly's white face and dark bruises, her beautiful eyes covered by closed lids.

'Hi sweetheart, are you awake?' Rick kissed her forehead.

'No.'

'Then open up. See what I have for you.'

'I can't. I feel a fool.' Keeping her eyes closed, she continued, 'I love you. I was wrong and I'm sorry, but I'm not giving up being a Ranger.'

She opened her eyes and looked at him.

'Fine by me sweetheart, a lesson learned my love.'

How come she could always twist him round her little finger?

What the hell, pram pushing could wait another year.

THOSE WERE THE YEARS

Hi there, I'm a touring caravan called Bailey.

I heard them say they are going to retire me. I'm to be banished from my spot, where I have stood for the past thirty years. If I could cry tears, I would fill a bucket in five minutes. I'm not worn out. I've given them good service, no leaks and no draught holes, four or five, comfortable beds. *And*, I've put up with all those cooking smells; she's a thrifty lady, doesn't believe in eating out.

He tried to set me on fire one year, when a pair of his model plane wings was left over the gaslight. And what about those bikes I've had wiggled through my narrow door and tied to my coat hooks?

I've been towed round England, Scotland, Wales and every country in Europe.

Never once did a tail wag, when he was bounding along the motorway at sixty miles an hour. It's all in the packing, so I heard him say; get the centre of gravity right, whatever that might mean.

Mind you, we did jack-knife in a muddy Welsh campsite and dent my left front corner. Gosh, did that hurt! So did the hammering to straighten it out.

I'm sounding all moans. There were the lovely hot days that followed near Harlech Castle. Heaven for me, she cooked outside.

I must mention one foggy, *pea soup* foggy, night in Scotland. They couldn't find the site. I was being shunted to a stop every few yards and the voices inside the car were getting louder. Suddenly I was swung into a lay-by and my aching body relaxed only when they fell into their bunks to sleep. I'm a martyr to the bumping treatment I get.

The next morning was a different world – blue sky, sun – and we were only yards away from the campsite! Halstead's Farm and Museum, at Hadrian's Wall. I won't go into what was said.

Later, I couldn't believe my windows when they brought a kitten inside me. It was a longhaired ginger tom with a white-ringed tail. It was half farm, half wild cat! Had they gone mad? They left it in a box on my table! I was very careful not to bump along the narrow roads, but that did depend on how skilful he was until we joined the motorway south.

Puss and I became great travelling partners over the next ten years, and he always sat on the table and looked out of the front window.

And of course there was the time...

What's that? I'm her lovely little home from home; I've got so many memories she can't do it. Is this a reprieve? They want to have me swung into the air, over the roof and land in the garden. They must be stark raving bonkers!

It's the only way, or I'm out on my tyres behind the first rag and bone van that comes along.

Bring on the lifting gear. I can't wait to be a summerhouse.

ALL FOR A TENNER

Young Jess couldn't believe it had happened.

'You're joking, Beth.'

'I'm not, love. Those rumours we heard? They're true. We're all being called to a meeting and you know what that means, closure!'

Jess's insides twisted with anxiety. What was she going to do? Ken worked in the storeroom; they had both worked for Woolies since leaving school.

'I've got to see Ken. If I'm wanted, say I'm in the loo.'

She hurried from the shop through the staff door that led into the warehouse, then stopped. If the shop was closing down why was there so much stock? Every shelf was full of Christmas toys, boxes of chocolates, crackers. There was enough to fill every Santa stocking in town.

Ken was loading a trolley with boxes of Christmas cards and rolls of wrapping paper. 'Have you heard?' she called, rushing over to him.

'I bloody well have. I can't believe it. Not a nod from the manager. The redundancy money will be a pittance, and that won't go far.'

'What about our wedding? How are we going to pay for it now?'

'Don't fret, Jess, we'll sort something out. This isn't going to stop us.'

She wanted to hug him, but it wasn't the place in front of the others. They usually gave her a wolf whistle whenever she came in, but not today. The men stood in groups, muttering, not doing any work until they knew what was what. Ken drew her to him behind the loaded trolley and kissed her.

She pulled away. 'Ken, they might see.'

He smiled, 'So what if they can? Management is too busy huddled someplace deciding our fate. They can't dismiss me for improper conduct if the rumours are true.'

'No, but –'

He kissed her forehead. 'Go back to your till. I'll see you at one o'clock in Nat's Café.'

*

The meeting was fraught, the Big Boss keeping a cheery face, but the worst was out. All stores were closing. Woolworth, one of England's established businesses' was closing forever.

Jeers of, 'Shame on you,' filled the open plan office. Over-riding this was the raised voices of, 'You can't do this!' and finally to angry shouts of, 'Bastards.'

Jess held on to Beth's arm, her legs turning to jelly, her heartbeat thumping like the death-drum.

'I'm going to faint. Can we go outside?'

Beth helped her through the crush of staff standing shocked to their core.

The fresh air cooled her face and Beth found a stool. 'Here, love, sit down and I'll get you a drink.'

Jess's mind was reeling. She had thought her job a sure bet and on that principle, Ken and she had bought a two bedroom apartment six months ago. How were they going to pay the mortgage now?

Beth handed her a cup of water and she sipped; then burst into tears.

'Don't cry, Jess. They're not worth it. We'll get another job. It's just the shock.' Tears filled her eyes and she fumbled in her pocket to find a hanky.

'What about my wedding: the dress, the flowers and the reception? Ken and I are paying for it all – our parents haven't got the money – their divorce fees took all that.

Beth patted her shoulder. 'You'll just have to cut corners a bit. Getting married is the main thing.'

She nodded, but it was to be her big day, the one time she wanted everything perfect, no expense spared.

'I'm seeing Ken lunchtime. I think I'll get a bit more fresh air, clear my head. Tell Boss Lady I've gone sick.'

She collected her coat and bag and walked along the street and sat on a wall by the memorial monument. She opened her shoulder-bag and took out her wedding list, but the items blurred with her tears. That beautiful lace gown was £600. There was no way they could pay that now. Bitter disappointment mingled with the fear of the uncertainty waiting in the wings – she had wanted that dress so much.

The cold wind blew through her and she started walking again. The sound of an ambulance siren made her look back, its blue light flashing as it swerved out of sight towards the hospital – some poor soul needed help, no doubt much more serious than her grumbles – her plight was just self-pity. She wandered into the Arcade, past the cheese shop, the Magician's Cavern, Esther's Boutique and finally stopped at the Oxfam window. There was the usual display of china tea sets, jewellery, a Monopoly game and a Nativity scene of a plastic Joseph, Mary and baby Jesus in a manger. As she stepped away a spotlight caught her eye shining on a trellis frame – draped from a clothes hanger was a white dress, so pure, so simple in style she couldn't take her eyes from it. It wasn't a wedding gown – just a short sleeved dress, scooped neckline, and the length would be just below the knees. Jess stared, her mind working on a thought so different from earlier.

The next moment she was inside. 'Could you tell me the size and price of the white dress, please?'

'Lovely isn't it dear. Just put it in the window half hour ago. Size twelve, it's new, so the price is eight pounds.'

'Could I try it on?'

'Of course you can. Pop into the changing room and I'll get it.'

Jess waited in her bra and pants until a hand waggled round the curtain.

'Take your time, we're not busy.'

Zipped up, she fluffed her hair and looked in the mirror. The dress was lined, the soft material hanging smooth over her slim figure. She pulled the curtain aside and went into the shop.

'That looks lovely on you. What about a rope of pearls.' The motherly woman rummaged in a box and brought out a long row and slipped them over Jess's head. 'Perfect, dear. Is the dress for anything special?'

'Well ...' Jess didn't want to tell a stranger her business, but the old lady was so nice. 'It may be my wedding dress. Have you heard about Woolies?'

'I've heard the rumours. Is it true then? Our Woolies finished, kaput?'

'I work there. We're all out, finished at Christmas. So my lovely wedding gown I've been saving for is not possible now. I thought maybe this would do.'

'Oh, it's perfect. Now, what about this nice blue coloured hat.' She flipped a wide brimmed creation trimmed with satin ribbon off a peg and set it on Jess's head. 'Why, that's just your colour with that lovely dark hair and it's a perfect match to your eyes.'

Jess went back into the cubicle and gazed at her reflection in the mirror. The transformation from the miserable girl of an hour ago was a miracle. She really did look a million – well a hundred – dollars.

'How much for all three?' she queried.

'For you dear, special price, a tenner the lot.'

'Thank you, you're very kind.'

Jess went into Nat's Café, a crumpled Tesco's bag bulging with her bargain finds. Her future husband, sitting tall above many of the other customers, even though he had his blond-haired head bowed, cradled a large china mug of steaming coffee. His hunched shoulders a similar sign of how she had felt sitting on the wall.

'Ken,' she waved to him across the room, 'It's going to be all right.'

She weaved her way to him, sat down, put her treasure trove on the floor and threw her arms around his neck.

'I've saved hundreds of pounds. We can do the same for you. Who needs a big reception, we can celebrate here in Nat's Café.'

Jess kissed him in full view of everyone.

'Happy Christmas, darling. We'll get through this – Woolies or no Woolies.'

THE GRANDFATHER CLOCK

A mellow chime echoes along the hallway. On the last midnight stroke, the pendulum door of a grandfather clock opens. White mist swirls out and starts to take form – Tom Buchannan's ghost is returning.

Tom is in his uniform, the newly earned sergeant stripes bright against the ragged and muddy khaki. He touches the fawn flowered wallpaper with fingers cut and scabbed with dried blood. His scuffed boots soundless, as he walks along the worn carpet runner. There is no need to open the parlour door; he can pass through. The room is just as he remembers it, and sitting in his armchair, slides his fingers through the cloth. The round table shines, the sofa set precisely at an angle to the fireplace. He looks for his pipe; of course, it wouldn't be here now. The curtains are drawn, is this in respect for him? Surely not, although today is his first anniversary of death on July first, nineteen-sixteen.

Tom moves to the Aspidistra, pleased to see it free of dust as his fingers pass through the leaf.

Amelia is upstairs.

She is his reason for coming back. The reason he cannot pass over until he has seen her one last time.

Tom counts thirteen stairs. When he had carried Amelia up them on their wedding night, they had laughed at superstition, calling them their lucky thirteen to heaven.

Amelia lies in the double bed on the left, her side from their first night, a daisy patterned nightdress buttoned to her throat and covering her arm to the wrist. Her breathing is soft. He remembers her little whimpers when she is dreaming. She always said they were happy moments to store away for a rainy day. God, she had needed them this past year.

Tom lies down beside her. Why couldn't he have been whole for just this one time? To hold her, feel the softness of her skin, the warmth of her lips. But it was not to be, he must be content just to watch her sleep.

The light comes early and Amelia awakes. She throws back the cover. Tom is shocked by her indifference. Can she not sense him? Has her love not been strong enough to feel he is there? She soaps her face at the washbasin. The oval shape is thinner and her cheeks pale. Is her life so much harder without him?

He follows her into his sons' bedroom and stands by the window. How they have grown. The three heads have his brown colouring and their heights tell him which are Gordon, Dougie and Roy. All three still sleep in the iron bedstead he had bought from a rag-and-bone man on his way home from the factory before the war. Their feet had only reached halfway down the mattress; now Gordon's almost touch the bedrail.

Watching them dress he wonders why they struggle to get into their clothes, then realises they are far too small. Why cannot Gordon's be passed down? In the stronger light he sees Amelia's dress is faded and the elbows are threadbare. Did Amelia not have enough money?

There is nothing his ghostly pockets can provide.

Things are not going well. Tom struggles with his conscious. Oats, grey without milk suffice for breakfast. Not a slice of bread to fill their hungry tummies.

After they had gone to school, Tom sits in his fireside chair to watch Amelia.

She fetches logs from the garden and piles them by the black iron range, then lifts the round lid with an angled handle. The flames flare as each log is dropped in and the fire comes to life. She waves red chapped hands in front of the grill.

He cannot feel the warmth, but to see her joy comforts him.

All morning he follows her: making the beds, scrubbing the front step. In the hall, Amelia stops at the grandfather clock – his wedding present to her – she runs her hands over its curved shape. Raising a finger to her lips, she kisses it and places it on the glass face. Suddenly, she leans her head on the rosewood panel and gulps of tears and sorrow escape from her shaking body. Tom is overwhelmed. He has longed for this day, to be with her, their final time together. He wants to take away happy memories. But real life is too practical. Fairy-tale endings belong in books.

Amelia does not eat at noon. Just drinks a pot of tea.

Tom pokes his head through the larder door. There are only a few essentials. How is she managing?

The clock chimes two and she puts more logs in the range, opens the oven door to test the temperature. A smile lightens her face and erases the lines on her forehead. Moving quickly she collects flour and other ingredients. Amelia did not weigh any, just tips them into a bowl and works with her fingers, rubbing fat into flour, adding sugar, currants, eggs and milk, then scoops the mixture into a tin. Testing the temperature one more time, she puts the tin inside and closes the door.

Tom senses contentment in her and his worry that all is not well lessens.

This kitchen is the centre of their world. For cooking, ironing and eating. For Gordon's christening, Dougie's joining the Scout Cubs, Roy's first steps into his outstretched arms. Amelia uses the table for sewing, the boys to read and draw pictures. A room full of memories. Amelia comes back to check her baking.

This brings him back to the 'now'. He must not waste his precious hours fretting. But he knows why he is so restless. It is anger. Anger for what has been taken from him.

The front door opens. His sons come in and with them, carried by the summer breeze, a hooting noise and raised voices, followed by rolling wagon wheels and the neighing of horses. Times are a-changing fast.

For Tom, there is no hunger as they eat their supper. But the sight of her fruitcake makes him want to lean forward and take a slice.

The early evening sunshine shafts through the kitchen window. Tom recognises the varnished toy trunk he made for Gordon. It gives him a good feeling to see his sons open it. Tom sits on the floor and watches Roy pushing a wooden train set on the linoleum covered boards; Dougie is sitting at the table with his paint-box colouring a horse; Gordon, searching through a book, turning the pages quickly. He stops, studies a page with a motor car picture. Does he want to work with them when he leaves school? Tom's anger returns. This is where he belongs, where he is needed.

Tom looks at the clock when his sons' bedtime goodnight calls end. He feels a tremor within, a warning...

He goes with Amelia into the garden. It's still the same: Amelia's little patch of grass inside borders of roses, daisies and lavender. The vegetable plot he loved to tend is not so neat. She breaks off a pink rose, smells the scent and pushes it into her fair hair. Lifting her face to the sky she closes her eyes.

Tom has resisted all day, but he cannot leave without holding her in his arms and kissing her lips. Neither can feel the touch, neither can express their love. Tom holds her a long time. It is not enough, this one day to store memories for evermore. He hopes she will find someone else to share her life. But the thought brings only jealousy of any man touching her as he had. But then, he can never come back.

The gas hisses, but the mantle is bright and Amelia sits close to the dying embers. She is knitting several colours, working a Fair Isle pattern.

She stops, rises from her chair and takes their framed wedding picture from the shelf above the range. It is their only one, for he and Amelia had avoided the photographer's lens. Holding it close she sways to and fro, gliding with little steps in a circle, tears spilling from her closed eyes. She is remembering, like him, another night, their first moments alone in this house. He had carried her into their bedroom, and they made love until the dawn. For today would have been their twelfth wedding anniversary. Amelia did not put the photo back, but pulls the gas chain and in the dimming light goes upstairs.

Tom lies with her one more time. His lifeless fingers ripple over her body. Her violet eyes remind him of summer pansies.

He doesn't want to go.

He cannot stay.

In the hall, the grandfather clock begins to chime.

One...Tom kisses her closed lids.

Two...Three...Four...He touches each boys head.

Five...Six...Seven...The stairs are taking him away.

Eight... He looks at the hole in his chest where his heart should have been.

Nine...The Somme – he had been in the first wave over the top.

Ten...The bastards didn't care, fodder for the cause.

Eleven...He mouths, 'Amelia – I don't want to go.'

Twelve...The mist fades from inside the grandfather clock.

Tom Buchannan's ghost is gone.

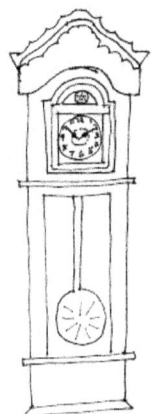

ABOUT THE AUTHOR

I have been a 'writer' since I was fifteen years old. I loved my English literature lesson when we were told to write a composition.

Most times we were given a theme. But my favourite time was when I had a blank page and could write what I pleased; adventures in wild jungles, ancient castles, Cornish smugglers' coves. Capturing foreign spies and out-witting aliens from space.

Now, I write Romantic Historical novels set in the Georgian/Regency era – a dashing hero rescuing a spirited heroine from the wicked Spanish sea captain.

I am always looking for a challenge. My new Kaleidoscope series of short stories, will, I hope bring a smile or a tear as you read.

I am a member of the Romantic Novelists' Association. At their Golden Anniversary Conference year I was thrilled to achieve third place in the Elizabeth Goudge annual writing award.

Go to: http://accenthub.com/2016/12/1264466/
for an insight into my research and recent releases

You can find out more about my work at:

www.julieroberts.me.uk

Facebook: @julieoroberts

Twitter: @julieoroberts

Exclusive Extract

As a thank you for purchasing this book, I am thrilled to share with you an Exclusive Extract from my latest release: The Hidden Legacy.

I do hope that you enjoy it.

Who is the mysterious Madame Lightfoot from Frederick's past?

*

On the death of her guardian, Frederick, Meredith Sanders inherits his art gallery in Ludgate Hill. This brings her closer to Blackfriars and Newgate Prison, the two places she most fears. Her ambition of becoming a renowned artist draws her into Frederick's criminal legacy and danger.

At first, businessman Adam Fox suspects Meredith of being involved in an art fraud relating to a missing Turner painting. Despite her fear of betrayal, she asks him for help as he is the only man she can trust.

If the painting is not returned to the Royal Academy before the Summer Exhibition, Adam may not be able to save her from the gallows.

And whatever her feelings for Adam, Meredith will not reveal the secrets of her own past...

For readers of Nicola Cornick, and Stephanie Laurens, an exciting new voice in Regency romance.

The story begins...

THE HIDDEN LEGACY

CHAPTER ONE

April 1815

This moment was the beginning of her new life.

Meredith stood in front of a building in Ludgate Hill. She owned every brick and room squeezed between a silversmith and a tailor's premises. From today it was her home, her art studio, and gallery. She wanted to dance and clap her hands, though such girlish behaviour would not be appropriate. But it was still a wonder that her beloved guardian, Frederick, had bequeathed it to her.

She stepped close to the window, which reflected her green eyes bright with happiness. A light breeze lifted a strand of dark hair as she rubbed her finger over a dust spot. The new easels had emptied her purse, but they had been worth every penny as they displayed her two favourite paintings, a river scene and a portrait of a boy.

The sound of bolts being drawn in the adjoining shops made her heart beat faster. Could she succeed in the art world? Would artists allow an un-sponsored, unprotected woman into their realm of canvas and oils? Enter studios where models were draped in only swathes of scarlet silk?

Going inside, she left the front door open. It presented a more welcoming entrance than a client having to knock. The dusty and dingy room of two weeks ago was now covered with unbleached linen panels. It had transformed the space into a light and airy gallery. In pride of place on the long wall was her painting of Frederick.

She picked up *The Times* and read the advertisement she had placed. It looked small and insignificant amongst so many others.

Artist of experience seeks pupils to tutor in the graces of drawing and painting.

Mondays and Wednesdays – 9am until noon.

Charge 5s.0d per morning.

Sanders Studio, Ludgate Hill.

Should she be sitting when a client arrived? She swept her skirt across a wooden chair and seated herself behind a spindly-legged desk that she had bargained fiercely for with a mean-faced trader at a flea market – but she loved the elegant tone it gave the gallery.

Fifteen minutes passed. She couldn't sit a moment longer and paced the length of the room, counting each step ... Thirty minutes! What would she do if no one came? Frederick had, in his will, provided her with an allowance which ought to cover her own expenses. But there was also Mrs Clements to provide for. It had only been proper to invite her to leave Harlington and come to London as her companion and housekeeper. Her tuition money would be essential to pay Mrs Clements' wages. And what about buying her art materials? If she sold a painting she would need to create another to replace it. Her plan to put aside a little money each quarter for emergencies was looking more than fanciful. Clearly being independent meant shouldering a lot of personal and household responsibilities.

Clattering horses' hooves sounded outside the window and Meredith hurried to see what was happening. A well-attired gentleman was lifting a little girl from a coach. A moment later he opened the inner gallery door and together they stepped inside.

Now that she could see him better, he was a very handsome gentleman. His dark hair touched the collar of his jacket and his eyes were the darkest of brown. He removed his hat, favoured a slight bow, and said, 'Good morning. My niece and I have come in answer to an advertisement regarding tuition. Would you please announce to the artist that Mr Fox and Miss Weston are here?'

This was not a good start. He thought she was an assistant? Her hands started to tremble and she clasped them tightly and prayed the dark dress she wore gave her a professional appearance.

She curtsied. 'You address the artist, sir.'

He stepped back. 'You! But you're a ...' he faltered, 'a lady, a very young lady!'

If this was the reaction she was going to get whenever a prospective client walked through the door, interviews would be extremely tedious. But she would not be intimidated by his words, she raised her head an inch and replied, 'I am Miss Meredith Sanders, at your service, sir. I can assure you I am qualified to tutor.'

Mr Fox gestured to the window. 'Come closer that I might see better a lady who recommends herself so highly.' Meredith bit her tongue. How many times had she been warned that her frank speaking would be her downfall? Was she now going to lose this client she so desperately needed?

'I beg your pardon sir, I meant no offence.'

Amusement tinged his voice as he repeated, 'I asked you to come nearer the light.'

The last thing she wanted to do was provoke a disagreement, so she stepped forward and said, 'This is a bright room, sir. However, I am happy to oblige you.'

His gaze started at her feet and moved upwards to her eyes, his expression revealing nothing of his thoughts.

'Tell me, how many of these paintings can I attribute to you?'

'All of them, sir.' Meredith kept her tone civil and swept her arm in a circle towards both long walls. 'I paint watercolour and oil, portrait and landscape.'

'Um,' was his only comment. 'Do you have a stool for my niece to sit on?'

Meredith indicated a wooden chair in the corner and the child sat down. Miss Weston's behaviour was demure, but there was an expectation in her, an excitement as she leant forward and watched her uncle's every move.

Mr Fox toured the room that was now her gallery, stopping to study first a landscape, then a charcoal sketch and finally the portrait of Frederick.

'Who is this?'

'My ... ' she hesitated, then the untruth left her lips, 'my late father, who was also my dearest friend.'

'Would you say this is a good likeness?'

Her grief, never far from the surface, returned. 'Oh, yes.' Her voice warmed, as it always did when she spoke of Frederick. 'He had the dearest of natures. Those lines beside his eyes were caused by laughter and his lips tilted up at the corners when he smiled. And he always wore the most brilliant of colours.' She was drawn into the painting, remembering the long summer days in his studio, how he had taught her to mix the oil paints, sketch an outline.

'I am much taken with your talent, Miss Sanders.'

She forced her memories aside, relieved to hear Mr Fox now viewed her with a more appreciative manner. Now that her initial fear had calmed, she could see his face was not so stern, his voice a more gentle tone. And his fine woollen green jacket fitted his broad shoulders to perfection. She let her gaze drift lower to the pale breeches and highly polished boots. Such an outfit could only come from the highest quality shops. A flutter of excitement ran down to her toes.

'Thank you, sir. Your compliment is a great encouragement.'

'How many pupils do you have? I would like Miss Weston to receive your full attention if she were to study here.'

'I have none at the moment, sir. You are my first client.'

Her palms were wet and her pulse raced. She didn't want to babble, but what else could she say to entice him to let his niece attend? 'I would not charge any more for private lessons, should Miss Weston be the only pupil.'

Mr Fox raised his brows. 'Ah. You are out to bargain with me?'

'Bargain with you, sir? I only meant ...' Her cheeks burned. Did he think she was trying to increase her fee?

Certainly she was in need of the tuition money, but she was not a scheming fraudster. No indeed!

'Sir, may I point out that I am not –'

He interrupted, a frown creasing his forehead. 'Where do you come from? Your accent is unfamiliar.'

Why did he want to know that? Did it matter? She had advertised offering art tuition, not applied to be a governess. But a sharp reply could go against her. Civility was surely the best action. 'I'm from Harlington, sir.'

'You're a country girl, of course. Where do you conduct your lessons?'

A spark of hope rose up. 'I have a studio at the back of this gallery.'

'I would like to see your references, before we proceed any further.'

'I can give you my personal references. My professional accomplishments are what you see on the walls.'

Meredith took three letters from her desk drawer, one from the Reverend Lyle, a second from Squire Norris, and the last from the Honourable Mrs Kilburn. She handed them to him.

'Each of these persons I have known for the past ten years.'

Mr Fox sat on her visitor's chair and opened the first letter.

What if she were unacceptable? Living under Frederick's protection she had never had a need to be interviewed, never to pay her own way. Her heart beat fast, as her dream of running this establishment, painting and selling her work, lay in what people like Mr Fox decided. To hide her nervousness she sat behind her desk and waited.

Minutes passed as he read, giving no indication by either manner or voice of how he was assessing her. He placed the letters on the desk.

'You have excellent references, Miss Sanders. Yet I have no friends or acquaintances that I could approach to vouch for you. By your own admission, you have come from Harlington, an area I know nothing of.'

This was another dilemma that had not occurred to her, that parents would be unwilling to leave their child in the care of a stranger.

He tapped his fingers on the desk. 'Do you have a companion living with you?'

'Yes, Mrs Clements is both my companion and housekeeper, sir. We have rooms above on two floors.'

'How long have you had her in your employ?'

'Mrs Clements came with me from Harlington. She was my father's housekeeper for twenty years.'

'May I ask you to draw a small sketch of my niece, to give me some assurance of your skill?'

Meredith drew in a breath and held it. He wanted her to draw with him watching? She released her breath, but her throat tightened and her hands suddenly had pins and needles. 'If that is your wish, sir, I will collect my sketch book and charcoal.'

He nodded. 'Do you want my niece to stay where she is?'

'Yes. Is a head and shoulders sufficient?'

'That would be quite sufficient, Miss Sanders.' His voice held no malice, no triumph, only the respectful request of a client.

Meredith's legs were trembling and her heartbeat was so loud in her ears she was sure Mr Fox could hear it as she walked into her studio. She closed the door and leant against it. His request was unexpected and frightening, but this was her chance to prove she was an artist, not just a *lady who paints*. She picked up her sketch book and charcoal, and mustered her inner bravado.

Mr Fox had moved her visitor's chair in front of his niece, sitting by the window.

'Thank you, Mr Fox. Now, Miss Weston, just look at one of the paintings on the wall behind me – excellent. This will take a few minutes, so please, keep very still.'

Meredith waited, her charcoal poised over the paper. Behind her she could feel Mr Fox's presence, caught the faint scent on his skin. Yet he was not threatening, instead there was a comfort in him being there. Her fingers relaxed and she studied the child. With quick strokes she drew the contours of her face, her lips, her nose, but it was her eyes sparkling with excitement that brought the sketch alive. Meredith finished the portrait with the tight fair curls peeking from under her cap and her shoulders covered with a lace collar.

Meredith turned and handed him her sketch book. Everything she hoped for now lay in Mr Fox's hand ....

....

Latest reviews of The Hidden Legacy:

A thrilling page-turner rich in romance, intrigue and adventure – *Nicola Cornick*

A perfectly pitched Regency romantic adventure. Engaging characters including a headstrong heroine, the right mix of historical background, romance, intrigue and skulduggery, and an interesting and unusual premise. I'll never visit an art gallery again without wondering! Well done, Julie Roberts, on her debut novel – *Amazon reader*

A rollicking Regency romantic adventure, with plenty of peril and flirtation – *Julie Cohen*

Very good book! I liked the story and the way it is written!! Romance, art, mystery and suspense are all in there! Couldn't stop reading it until the last page!!

Amazon reader

This is a rollercoaster of a novel full of adventure, passion and the righting of wrongs. At the centre of it is Meredith Sanders, a woman before her time, and Adam Fox, a complicated yet compassionate hero. Julie Roberts' attention to detail is second-to-none and she brings the time about which she is writing vividly to life.'

Claire

I've thoroughly enjoyed reading this book. The story draws you in and before you know it, you're turning the last page. Very much looking forward to the next book Julie publishes – hopefully I won't be waiting long!!

Amazon reader

Discover more about The Hidden Legacy https://www.accentpress.co.uk/the-hidden-legacy.